JF GRIFFIN
Griffin, Molly Beth, author.
Party time

SCHOOL SIDEKICKS
PARTY TIME

by Molly Beth Griffin

illustrated by Colin Jack

PICTURE WINDOW BOOKS
a capstone imprint

TABLE OF CONTENTS

Chapter 1
A SPECIAL WEEK 7

Chapter 2
THE GOODBYE 13

Chapter 3
NEW KINDS OF FUN .. 21

SCHOOL SIDEKICKS

These five friends live within the walls, nooks, and crannies of an elementary school. They learn alongside kids every day, even though the kids don't see them!

STELLA

Stella is a mouse. She loves her friends. She also loves children and school! She came into the school on a cold winter day. She knew it would be her home forever. Her favorite subjects are social studies and music. She is always excited for a new day.

BO

Bo is a parakeet. He is a classroom pet. The friends let him out of his cage so they can play together. Bo loves to read. He goes home with his teacher on weekends, but he always comes back to school to see his friends.

DELILAH

Delilah is a spider. She has always lived in the corners of the school. She is so small the children never notice her, but she is very smart. Delilah loves math and computers and hates the broom.

NICO

Nico is a toad. He used to be a classroom pet. A child forgot to put him back into his tank one day. Now he lives with his friends. The whole school is his home! He can be grumpy, but he loves science and art. Since Nico doesn't have fingers, he paints with his toes!

GOLDIE

Goldie is a goldfish. She is very wise. The friends ask her questions when they have a big choice to make. She gives good advice and lives in the media center.

A SPECIAL WEEK

It was the last week of school, and Stella the Mouse couldn't believe her luck!

"It's just one fun thing after another!" she told her friends. "And I love parties!"

On Monday, Stella sang in the music concert. All the parents sat and listened.

Under the bleachers, Stella sang her heart out. Her friends cheered.

On Tuesday, Nico the Toad hung his best painting in the hallway art show.

The friends looked at all the children's beautiful drawings, paintings, and sculptures.

"Amazing!" Nico said. He painted all their ribbons blue.

On Wednesday, Delilah the Spider watched over the math competition.

She answered almost every question correctly, even if no one heard her.

On Thursday, Bo the Parakeet joined the spelling bee. He misspelled the word *ankylosaurus*.

"It's even one of my favorite dinosaurs!" he said. His friends hugged him tight.

On Friday, the friends watched the children play outside at the school picnic.

Stella didn't think life could get any better.

THE GOODBYE

But then, something horrible happened. When the picnic ended and the children headed for the buses, the teachers went too. Every single one of them.

The teachers stood on the sidewalk. They waved to the children as the buses drove away.

The children waved back.

"Goodbye, goodbye!" they called.

"Have a good summer!" the teachers called.

"Oh no!" said Stella. "The children are going away? Forever?"

"Summer?!" said the friends.

The teachers walked back inside the school. Stella sniffed. She thought her heart would break.

"What about me?" said Bo. "Will I have to go home with the teacher for the summer?"

Stella gasped. "Let's go ask Goldie."

The friends rushed to the media center. They could always ask Goldie when they had a problem. She knew what to do.

"Goldie, it's summer. The children have gone. Will Bo have to go away all summer too?" Stella asked.

Goldie swam in a circle.

"Blub, blub," she said. That meant no. At least they thought it did.

"No?" said Bo. "I will get to stay? Or at least, visit?"

"Blub," said Goldie. That meant yes.

"Yay!" said Stella. "But Goldie, will the school be empty all summer?"

"Blub, blub," said Goldie.

"Oh, good!" Stella said.

She was relieved, but she had no idea what summer would bring.

Stella missed the children already. She wanted her happy routines to go on forever.

She loved learning with the children every day. She loved helping the teachers.

What would she do every day now? Why did things have to change at all?

Chapter 3

NEW KINDS OF FUN

The next morning, loud music woke up Stella and her friends. Stella followed the music, her friends right behind her.

The teachers were back and had turned on the radio. They were cleaning out their classrooms.

"Watch out!" said Delilah.

The broom rushed past. It was moving really fast. Then the mops zoomed by!

The custodians had to deep clean the school while the children were away.

The clearing out and cleaning up went on for days. The friends helped when they could.

They stayed out of the way when brooms and mops came by. One time a huge machine whirred past to wax the floors. Yikes!

Soon the teachers were gone too. The friends didn't know what to do. But the school quickly filled with people again.

The building buzzed with classes and camps. There were so many fun things to try.

Stella discovered marching band.

Nico tried out pottery class.

Delilah learned to jump rope.

Bo's teacher taught summer school classes, so he was at school a lot. Bo went to book clubs. And story times. And writing camp!

The friends had fun trying new things. They'd been so worried about summer. Now they didn't want summer to end!

Before long the teachers came back. They planned their lessons. They organized and decorated their rooms. The animal friends secretly pitched in.

Nico made the bulletin boards pretty. Delilah sorted school supplies. Bo alphabetized books.

Stella scurried around, helping everyone. She wanted everything to be perfect for the children when they returned.

Summer had been more fun than the friends had expected. But nothing was more fun than a new school year!

TALK ABOUT IT

1. The last week of school often includes fun activities. What is your favorite activity at the end of the school year?

2. Which one of the School Sidekicks are you most like? Why?

3. The animals always ask Goldie for advice. Whom do you go to for advice? Why?

WRITE ABOUT IT

1. Write about a summer class that you would enjoy taking.

2. Make a list comparing how you felt on the first day of school and on the last day.

3. Write a short story about what you think teachers do during the summer.

MOLLY BETH GRIFFIN

Molly Beth Griffin is a writing teacher at the Loft Literary Center in Minneapolis, Minnesota. She has written numerous picture books (including *Loon Baby* and *Rhoda's Rock Hunt*) and a YA novel (*Silhouette of a Sparrow*). Molly loves reading and hiking in all kinds of weather. She lives in South Minneapolis with her partner and two kids.

COLIN JACK

Colin Jack has illustrated several books for children, including *Little Miss Muffet* (Flip-Side Rhymes), *Jack and Jill* (Flip-Side Rhymes), *Dragons from Mars*, *7 Days of Awesome*, and *If You Happen to Have a Dinosaur*. He also works as a story artist and character designer at DreamWorks Studios. Colin splits his time living in California and Canada with his wife and two children.

PLENTY OF SIDEKICK FUN!

Discover more at
www.capstonekids.com

School Sidekicks is published by
Picture Window Books, a Capstone Imprint
1710 Roe Crest Drive, North Mankato, Minnesota 56003
www.mycapstone.com

Library of Congress Cataloging-in-Publication Data
Names: Griffin, Molly Beth, author. | Jack, Colin, illustrator.
Title: Party time / by Molly Beth Griffin ; illustrated by Colin Jack.
Description: North Mankato, Minnesota : Picture Window Books, [2019]
| Series: Picture Window Books. School sidekicks |

Summary: The last week of school is party time for the students
and teachers, but Stella the Mouse, Nico the Toad, Delilah the Spider,
and Bo the Parakeet are a little concerned about what happens
after the students leave for the summer—Bo will go home with
his human, but the others are worried that they will be
bored and hungry if the school shuts down.

Identifiers: LCCN 2018037919| ISBN 9781515838890 (hardcover) |
ISBN 9781515838937 (ebook pdf)

Subjects: LCSH: Animals—Juvenile fiction. | Elementary schools—
Juvenile fiction. | School buildings—Juvenile fiction. | CYAC: Animals—
Fiction. | Schools—Fiction. | School buildings—Fiction.

Classification: LCC PZ7.G8813593 Par 2019 | DDC 813.6 [E] —dc23
LC record available at https://lccn.loc.gov/2018037919

Book design by: Ted Williams
Shutterstock: AVA Bitter, design element throughout,
Oleksandr Rybitskiy, design element throughout

Printed and bound in the United States of America.
PA49